Hillert, Margaret
          Four good friends

E
HIL

69A0164

Hillert, Margaret
          Four good friends

E
HIL

69A0164
TITLE

DATE DUE	BORROWER'S NAME	ROOM NUMBER
NOV. 16	Kelly V	103
OCT. 1 4 1982	Lauren	101
FEB. 1 3 1985	Mary Beth	103
MAR 1 3 1986	Howacz	242

Four Good Friends

A Follett JUST Beginning-To-Read Book

Four Good Friends

Margaret Hillert
Illustrated by Krystyna Stasiak

FOLLETT PUBLISHING COMPANY
Chicago

80-32

Library of Congress Cataloging in Publication Data

Hillert, Margaret.
  Four good friends.

  (Follett just beginning-to-read books)
  SUMMARY: A retelling of the Grimm fairy tale in which four animal friends, in search of a place to live, scare robbers from a house in the forest and decide to live there together.
  [1. Fairy tales. 2. Folklore—Germany] I. Stasiak, Krystyna. II. Title.
PZ8.H5425Fo   398.2′45′0943 [E]   79–26083
ISBN 0–695–41356–2 lib. bdg.
ISBN 0–695–31356–8 pbk.

Library of Congress Catalog Card Number: 79–26083

International Standard Book Number: 0–695–41356–2 Library binding
                                           0–695–31356–8 Paper binding

First Printing

I can not work.
No one wants me.
I have to go away.
Away, away, away.

Oh, my. Oh, my.
You do not look good, little one.
Why?
What is it?

I can not work.
No one wants me.
I am no good.

7

Come. Come.
I like you.
You can come with me.

See here now.
We will go away.
We will find something.

9

What is this?
What have we here?
You are a big one.

I can not run.
I can not work.
What will I do now?
Where will I go?

You are big.
Big, big, big.
You can help us.

You can come with us.
We want you.
Come with us to see
what we can find.

My, how pretty you are.
But, what is it?
Can we help?

I am no good, I guess.
No one wants me.
What am I to do?

Do you want to come with us?
We like you.
We want you.

Look here.
A little house.
Is this what we want?

17

Have a look.
What do you see?
What is in this house?

19

I see a man.
I see two.
I see three.

We want to see, too.
Do it like this.
Here we go.
Up and up and up.

24

Oh, oh, oh!
Oh, my. Oh, my!
Oh, look at that!

25

Get out! Get out!
It is not good for us here.
Get away! Get away!
Run, run, run.

27

Now that is funny.
What did we do?
But come in here.
It looks good in here.

29

Now we have a house.
We have something to eat.
We do not have to work.
We are happy.

31

Margaret Hillert, author of many Follett JUST Beginning-To-Read Books, has been a first-grade teacher in Royal Oak, Michigan, since 1948.

Four Good Friends uses the 61 words listed below.

a	get	man	that
am	go	me	this
and	good	my	three
away	guess		to
		no	too
big	happy	not	two
but	have	now	
	help		up
can	here	oh	us
come	house	one	
	how	out	want(s)
did			we
do	I	pretty	what
	in		where
eat	is	run	why
	it		will
find		see	with
for	like	something	work
funny	little		
	look(s)		you